James Wills

The Mind

Anatiposi

James Wills

The Mind

Reprint of the original.

1st Edition 2023 | ISBN: 978-3-38230-558-1

Anatiposi Verlag is an imprint of Outlook Verlagsgesellschaft mbH.

Verlag (Publisher): Outlook Verlag GmbH, Zeilweg 44, 60439 Frankfurt, Deutschland
Vertretungsberechtigt (Authorized to represent): E. Roepke, Zeilweg 44, 60439 Frankfurt, Deutschland
Druck (Print): Books on Demand GmbH, In de Tarpen 42, 22848 Norderstedt, Deutschland

THE MIND;

ITS CAPABILITIES AND CULTIVATION,

BEING THE

SUBSTANCE OF A LECTURE

DELIVERED IN THE READING ROOM OF THE

CALVER AND STONY MIDDLETON

MUTUAL IMPROVEMENT SOCIETY,

BY

JAMES WILLS,

AUTHOR OF " AN ADDRESS ON RELIGIOUS TRAINING," "EXPOSITION OF PSALM XIX.,"
" LETTER TO YOUNG CHRISTIANS," " HISTORICAL AND SENTIMENTAL CARDS," &c.

SHEFFIELD:

PRINTED BY ROBERT LEADER, Jun., INDEPENDENT OFFICE.
SOLD BY H. PEARCE, OLD HAYMARKET ;
BY J. GOODWIN AND J. GRATTON, BAKEWELL; AND ALL BOOKSELLERS.
1859.

PREFACE.

I delivered the following lecture on Wednesday, March 9th, 1859, at Calver. On that occasion I omitted some concluding portions of the lecture, fearing that the subject was not at all interesting; but from the remarks of some highly respectable and literary persons, I found that my fears were groundless. Being requested to put it into a permanent form, that those who heard it, and others who did not, might have an opportunity of perusing it quietly at their own homes, I have ventured on its publication, with a sincere desire that many may be stimulated to attend promptly to the cultivation of their minds. It has been my study to make the subject as inviting and popular as I possibly could. In order to this, my illustrations have been somewhat redundant. I hope that the language employed will be found clear and intelligible to the general reader. If but one individual be benefited by its perusal, I shall feel myself amply repaid.

Hollow Brook Cottage, Eyam,
    July 5th, 1859.

LECTURE ON THE MIND:

ITS CAPABILITIES AND CULTIVATION.

LADIES AND GENTLEMEN,

The subject of this evening's lecture is the Mind:
its Capabilities and Cultivation. An able writer on the
subject of " Mental and Moral Science," has observed
that " the mind of man must be allowed to be the
noblest production of Almighty power; it deserves,
therefore, our closest study." An American writer remarks that " the HUMAN MIND is the brightest display of
the power and skill of the Infinite Mind with which we
are acquainted. It is created and placed in this world
to be educated for a higher state of existence. Here
its faculties begin to unfold, and those mighty energies
which are to bear it forward to unending ages, begin to
discover themselves." Yes—the mind, with its all but
infinite capabilities, like the concealed beauties of the
flower in the bud, lies enfolded in the embryo man;
but, as time rolls on, it becomes expanded, and bursts
forth from its infant chrysalis, and operates upon external objects, bringing about results which are truly
astonishing. As to the *essence* of mind we are, and per-

B

haps ever will be, in ignorance. As to its nature—it is that immaterial, immortal, and " mysterious principle within us, which constitutes the permanent subject of various phenomena, or properties, differing essentially from those which matter exhibits." But, while we know much more of matter from the uniform effects or results produced by certain combinations, yet, concerning the essence of both *matter and mind* we are, and must remain, shut up in profound ignorance. It is very humbling to the pride and vanity of the human heart, to feel incapable of coming to a correct knowledge of the essence of matter.

We become acquainted with the properties of matter through the medium of the external senses; and of the operations, feelings, and affections or emotions of the mind by our consciousness. The properties of mind are altogether opposed to and different from matter. Matter is divisible. Mind is indivisible. Matter has figure or extension, colour, &c. Mind has not figure, colour, extension. We arrive at the knowledge of the various properties, feelings, and emotions of the mind by observation. We are either directly conscious of them ourselves, or we have indirectly observed them in others.

The mind, then, is an *indivisible essence*, the offspring of the uncreated, self-existent, and infinite Being, upon which He has impressed His own immateriality and immortality; intimately and mysteriously associated with matter in its sphere of conscious observation and operation. That principle which, after the tenement of clay which it now inhabits, shall have returned to commingle with its native element in the tomb, shall bloom in eternal youth and vigour. It is that which at once holds communion with God, angels, and men. It does not come within the limits and design of a popular lecture to descant upon the various phenomena of mind, internally and externally considered, yet it may not be considered out of place to give some general view of the different orders and classes of the external and internal affections of the mind as they have been arranged by the celebrated Dr. Brown. I shall then proceed to make some remarks on the different inlets to the mind, and some of those emotions and feelings. Before giving the arrangement of the mental phenomena, it must be premised that much that is infinitely mysterious to us exists in the doctrine of the connexion between matter and mind. There is not, however, anything more peculiarly mysterious in the influence which mind has upon matter, or matter upon mind, than there is in the influence which matter exerts upon matter. How wonderful it is that, in the case of odoriferous plants, emitting their infinitesimal particles, coming in contact with the olfactory nerves, the effect of which is a change in the state of that organ, which is necessary in this instance to the sensation of smell. The *why* and *wherefore* can only be given by the Infinite. For reasons known only to himself, God has placed this boundary to man. In the meanest production of the Deity,—if I may be allowed the expression,—there is a height, a depth which no finite capacity can reach. And when the boasting materialist fancies that he has fully acquainted himself with the reasons for the various phenomena of the universe, he has got no further than to perceive that similar states similarly acted upon, the result is similar effects; or that the same body, in a similar state, produces the same or similar effects upon bodies in a similar state. But why, and for what reason, *he knows not.* Men are chafed and filled with chagrin and hatred of God, and sink into materialism as a last resort, for no other reason than they cannot grasp the Infinite. I confess that I cannot muster charity enough to believe that they are really learned or great men. I shall now proceed to give the late Dr. Brown's tabulated view of the mental phenomena :—

DIVISION I.
THE EXTERNAL AFFECTIONS OF THE MIND.

ORDER I.	ORDER II.
The less definite External Affections.	*The more definite External Affections.*
Class I.	Class I.
Appetites, such as Hunger, Thirst, &c.	Sensations of Smell.
Class II.	Class II.
Muscular Pains.	Sensations of Taste.
Class III.	Class III.
Muscular Pleasures.	Sensations of Hearing.
	Class IV.
	Sensations of Touch.
	Class V.
	Sensations of Sight.

DIVISION II.

THE INTERNAL AFFECTIONS OF THE MIND.

ORDER I.	ORDER II.
Intellectual States of Mind.	*Emotions; such as Love, &c.*
CLASS I.	CLASS I.
Simple suggestions. Suggestions of resemblance, contrast, contiguity.	Immediate emotions.
	CLASS II.
CLASS II.	Retrospective emotions.
Relative suggestions, or feelings of relations.	Species I.
	Retrospective emotions, having relation to others.
Species I.	Species II.
Relations of co-existence, position, resemblance, degree, proportion, comprehensiveness.	Retrospective emotions, having reference to ourselves.
	CLASS III.
Species II.	Prospective emotions.
Relations of succession.	

I shall now proceed to make some remarks on the second part of the External affections, or Inlets of the Mind.—These are usually termed the FIVE SENSES.

The external senses must not be considered as the powers of the mind; but as the expressions or indications of its powers, and its instruments or agents in conveying information to *it*, and also of conveying information to others.

No machinery or mechanism was ever at once so transcendently simple and well-ordered, as a whole, and, at the same time, so complex in its several parts, as the external organization of the mind, or the separate and combined external senses. Were we more closely to study these phenomena than we are accustomed, every one of us would find that he carried about with him a universe, as replete with the indications and proofs of the existence of the Infinite Jehovah as the world in which we live, and the universe itself of which we form a part.

We need not scale the heights above, nor dive into the depths beneath, neither need we take our seat in some particular part of the heavens in order to have overwhelming views and proofs of the power, majesty, and glory of God. We carry them about with us; yea, from the cradle to the grave.

We must now proceed to make some remarks upon some of the sensations which are produced by the external senses or inlets of the mind.

I. THE SENSE OF HEARING.—And, first, we shall notice the organ of hearing; and, second, some of its sensations.

The ear, or auricle, is a most delicate and complicated organ, fully adapted to answer all the great purposes of social intercourse, and the beneficent intentions of the Almighty.

The ears, in human beings, consist, first, of the external ear; second, an internal cavity of bone, which is furnished with a great number of winding passages, formed within the temporal bone; third, a strong transparent membrane, which is stretched across the passage just named, and so separates the two other parts from each other. This membrane is styled the tympanum, i.e., the drum of the ear. " By this membrane the vibrations of the air are received from the external ear, and are transmitted through the canals or passages called the labyrinth, to the auditory nerve, which is formed into a beautiful expansion." The impressions thus made upon the tympanum are conveyed by the auditory nerve to the brain, and the sensation of hearing is the immediate result.

How are these sensations produced? The answer is—that the equilibrium of the air is disturbed whenever any one speaks, or a bell is rung, or a gun is fired, &c., just the same as when a boy throws a stone or other hard substance into a pool of water, the effect of which is the describing of a great number of concentric circles. Now, when the air is thrown into a tremulous or vibratory state, and the ear situated within the reach or influence of these undulations, a vivid sensation of sound is produced. These atmospheric concentric circles, so to speak, strike the tympanum, and proceed through the medium of the auditory nerve, to be conveyed to the brain.

It is this sense which constitutes us capable of deriving pleasure from music. By it we become acquainted with the thoughts and emotions of others when orally expressed.

II. SENSE AND SENSATION OF SIGHT.—We shall first briefly describe the visual organs; and secondly, make some remarks on some of the sensations of sight.

First, the organ itself. We are informed that " the

eye is situated in a circular orbit, and composed of transparent substances, called humours, of various refractive densities, viz.—the aqueous, crystalline, and vitreous humours. The first refraction takes place on the surface of what is called the convex cornea of the eye, which receives the rays of light, converges and transmits them to the aqueous humour, a transparent fluid situated between the cornea and the crystalline humour. The pupil, or perforation in the centre of the iris, admits of the transmission of the rays from the aqueous humour to the crystalline lens, by which they are again refracted and transmitted to the vitreous humour, in which is placed the retina, or net-like expansion of the optic nerve." These several refractions of rays of light produce the image of the object from which they proceed, upon the retina.

What a display of the wisdom and beneficence of the Divine Being do we discover in the organs of vision! Consider their situation and adaptation to the purposes which they are intended to serve. Paley, in his Natural Theology, remarks, that " Were there no example in the world of contrivance, except the eye, it would be alone sufficient to the conclusion which we draw from it, as to the necessity and existence of an intelligent Creator. Its coats and humours, constructed as the lenses of a telescope, are constructed for the refraction of the rays of light to a point, which forms the proper action of the organ : the provision, in its muscular tendons, for turning its pupil to the object, similar to that which is given to the telescope by screws, and upon which power of direction in the eye, the exercise of its office, as an optical instrument, depends : the further provision for its defence, for its constant lubricity and moisture, which we see in its socket and its lids, in its gland, for the secretion of the matter of tears, its outlet or communication with the nose for carrying off the liquid after the eye is washed with it ; these provisions compose altogether an apparatus, a system of parts, a preparation of means, so manifest in their design, so exquisite in their contrivance, so successful in their issue, so precious and so infinitely beneficial in their use, as, in my opinion, to bear down all doubt that can be raised upon the subject."*

III. SENSE OF TOUCH.—As in the former senses, we shall in this notice, first, the organ or sense itself; and secondly, some of its sensations.

First, The Organ. This covers the entire body. It is thought that the nervous papillæ of the skin are the inlets of the sensations of touch or feeling.

Many and exceedingly curious are the opinions of such men as Reid, Brown, Stewart, &c., upon the different kinds of sensations which the sense of Touch excites or produces ; but we cannot introduce them into a lecture like the present.

Suffice it to say, that it connects the whole of the body with the brain. It differs, in this respect, from the other senses. Whenever a part of the body comes in

* pp. 81—82.

contact with any substance, communication immediately takes place with the brain, and we are informed of what has occurred by the peculiar sensation produced. Were the nervous membrane as extensive as the world, or did it reach the sun, an impression made upon it at the antipodes or at the sun would be instantly communicated to the mind. Just in the same way as information is conveyed by the electric telegraph from England to America, &c.

IV. SENSE OF SMELL.—For the purposes of distinguishing our food, enjoying the fragrance of flowers, and of avoiding many things which would otherwise be deleterious to us, the Great Creator has been pleased to furnish man, in common with other animals, though to a less extent than most, with the sense of smell.

The infinitesimal odour of the rose, musk, &c., is borne along the agitated strata of the atmosphere until it comes in contact with the olfactory nerves, and thus the sensation of smell is produced. We are told there is a set of nerves distributed through the delicate and very sensible nervous membrane, which lines the cavities of the nostrils and the senses with which they communicate. They arise from the brain in a triangular form, and, passing over the frontal bone, are conducted to each side of the nostrils, and spread out in numerous and minute ramifications on the nervous membrane just named.

In order that this delicate and exquisite piece of machinery may be preserved from injury, it is defended by the bones of the nose, which are admirably adapted to answer this end.

In this, as in all other things, we see an infinitely gracious adaptation of means to ends.

V. SENSE OF TASTE.—The organs of this sense show in an admirable manner the paternal care of the Deity, and the provision He has made for the vital interests of his creatures. The surface of the tongue is covered with nervous papillæ. It is thought that these nervous papillæ " exist within the substance of the mucous membrane which lines the palate." What a display of infinite wisdom and beneficence do we discover here! To what a number of infinitely diversified dangers are we exposed, which, were it not for the guard which the Almighty has placed at the entrance of the canal for respiration, and that of the alimentary one, would speedily put a termination to our existence. Let us adoringly admire the wisdom and benevolence of God in thus giving and disposing these several inlets of the mind.

Having thus directed your attention to the inlets of the mind, together with some observations on the mysterious and inexplicable nature of the union of matter and mind ; and the infinite wisdom which has been displayed in the whole of the physical and intellectual machinery, I shall next consider some of the properties or qualities of the mind peculiarly so, such as distinguish man from the brute, and at once shew that *he* is a moral agent ; from which it will not be difficult to ascertain

what his design and destiny are. The moral susceptibilities of the mind are original, and are not the result
of observation : they are perfectly distinct from the intellectual powers.

Man is capable of reasoning out a proposition, and
of forming a judgment concerning the actions of men, of
approving of some as being virtuous, and of discarding or
disapproving of others as being vicious. These moral
emotions and susceptibilities show most distinctly that
man is in a state of moral discipline, and a subject of
the great Moral Governor of the universe. When these
great moral susceptibilities of our nature are cultivated
aright, we become reflections of the endearing charac-
ters or expressions of the Deity, and all the treasures of
the universe seem to be opened to us, to which we are
invited to come, that our minds may be enriched, our bodies refreshed, and our happiness abundantly increased.

It is when these internal affections of our mental con-
stitution are under the control and guidance of true religion, that our minds become expanded and strengthened, and what is acquired is turned to profitable ac-
count. I would remark too, that it is of vaster importance
to have a well-regulated state of the passions and emotions, as a ground-work of mental culture, than we are
apt to suppose. For a man to throw the bridle over the
head of an infuriated steed, is the sure way to suffer con-
sequences of the most fatal character. In like manner,
if a man's passions and the natural tendencies of his
depraved heart be not kept under moral restraint, all ef-

forts, however great, complex, and numerous they may be, for the benefit of such a man, must prove abortive. As nothing can subdue the turbulent passions of our nature so completely as religion, I conjure you not to pour contempt upon the inspired volume ; but, on the contrary, to cultivate an enlightened acquaintance with its principles and maxims.

I do most unhesitatingly aver that if religion will not prepare the mental soil, and expand and strengthen all our intellectual powers, nothing will. I am aware that all learned men are not good men, neither all religious men learned men; but it by no means follows hence that it is not in the nature of true religion to produce the results we have been considering.

PART II.

THE CAPABILITIES OF THE MIND.

These are beyond our comprehension. We may say of them what we are constrained to say concerning the mysteries of Providence, that we know but in part; and how very small a part! We know something about mind from its expressions. It is capable of holding familiar intercourse with worlds that are removed from us thousands of millions of miles in the immensity of space. It can take note of the regularity of the motions of the heavenly bodies, calculate with accuracy solar, lunar, and sidereal eclipses.

It wings its flight from this terrestrial globe to other worlds, circumscribes and weighs them in the balances of mathematical rectitude. With the various data of which it is in possession, it can ascertain the angles and accurately measure the distances, and ascertain the constituents of their several atmospheres. The electric Prometheus has, as it were, been bound or confined within certain limits, in order to make it subservient to all the uses and advantages of civilised life. The electric fluid which, when unrestrained by art or the will of the Infinite, splits trees, fires ships, houses, arsenals; destroys men and beasts, and clothes the sky with its awful glare, and fills the souls of many with dire consternation,—is used as a speaking medium even by comparative children. The mind makes use of it to give expression of its thoughts and emotions to the inhabitants of near and remote countries. The inhabitants of New York are summoned to attention in a moment; and the thoughts and intentions of merchants and others in this country are disclosed to the Americans with the rapidity of lightning.

Look at the consociating power of the mind also in the varied arts of civilised life. See how the productions of one country are made subservient to the good of another. Its Herculean efforts in this particular are truly astonishing.

If we look at its capabilities in the infinite variety of chemical combinations, we shall be struck with the resources which are at its command for the benefit of the husbandman, artisan, and professional man. The faded glories of ancient Greece, Rome, Egypt, and that country which is sacred to the memory of the devoted Christian, by the footprints of the Redeemer, of prophets, apostles, martyrs, and confessors : all bear testimony to the greatness and undying energy of the *mind*. Our own highly-favoured country, in the innumerable changes which it has undergone, before and since its invasion by Cæsar, presents to our view most striking proofs of the gigantic powers of the mind.

The tenacity with which the mind keeps information concerning the past, present, or future anticipations, is well worthy of notice.

History furnishes not a few instances of persons of

extraordinary memories. It is reported of Seneca that he could recite and rehearse backwards 2000 verses without missing a syllable.

The great Mithridates, who governed twenty-three nations, all of different languages, could hold familiar intercourse with all in their several languages.

Dr. Wallis once extracted the cube root of the number three, to thirty places of decimals, by his memory alone. An Italian, of the name of Maglia Bethi, was a man of such extraordinary powers of retaining what he had read and heard, that he could at any time give the chapter, section, and page, and quote correctly from any of the very numerous authors he had read. A gentleman is reported to have tested the strength of his memory in the following manner :—He lent him a long manuscript which he was about to publish, and after it had been returned, called upon him soon afterwards, pretending he had lost it, and desired him to write as much of it as he could remember, when, to his very great surprise, he wrote it over accurately as it was in the manuscript.

M. Euler, the celebrated mathematician, by his intense application to study, lost his sight. Yet, such was the tenacious grasp of his memory that he composed his " Elements of Algebra," " The Inequalities of the Planetary Motions," a work which required immense and complicated calculations. He could repeat the Æneid of Virgil from beginning to end, and indicate the first and last line of every page of the edition he used.

Such is the mind's storehouse. And yet such is the power it possesses of discrimination and selection, that all the things which are perceived through the medium of the external senses, appear to be so classified and arranged that they are used singly, or in combination, just as circumstances require. This is a wonderful power of the mind, and discovers itself in infancy, acquires strength and vigour in manhood, and is unabated even in old age. Let us now consider the retrospective and suggestive powers of the mind. *Retrospective powers or emotions* of the mind are those which are occasioned by some circumstance which has transpired. Anger, for instance, is the displeasure which is excited within us by any supposed or real injury done either to ourselves or to others whom we love, or for whom we feel interested. When we have received benefits from any individual, this circumstance excites the emotion of gratitude. The atmosphere of obligation surrounds us, and our gratitude should ever be excited by it. In a well regulated mind, day and night, the seasons, the productions of the earth, and the capacity to enjoy them, call forth gratitude to God. The mind can turn back upon the past, and hold communion with the numberless mercies of God. It is this power of the mind which enables it to take cognisance of the past; and to hold the most familiar intercourse with the magnificent splendour of bye-gone days.

The suggestions of the *mind*. The laws of suggestion are said to be three, viz. :—Resemblance, contrast, and contiguity. Without going into any metaphysical minutiæ on this head, we shall consider suggestions popularly.

External objects suggest, recal, or reproduce certain affections or emotions. You see the tear trickling down the cheek of the sorrowing mother, as she glances at the toys of her departed babe. The noise of the restless waves of the ocean suggests to the fatherless and the widow, the shipwrecked husband and father. Trees, streams, lakes, rivers, seas, and oceans,—yea, the wide world itself, and the innumerable worlds and systems which revolve in space—are all suggestive to the mind of the dread majesty and glory of Jehovah.

The art of printing in all its various forms, giving expression to the thoughts of individuals in all the languages of civilised nations, giving permanency to thought, speaking in silence, conversing with the past in the page of history, must be considered as a wonderful achievement of *mind*. To make twenty-four signs or letters the means of conveying, in their several combinations, thousands of distinct emotions and thoughts, is no trifling affair. Add to this that some minds can give expression of their sentiments, &c., in many languages, employing different symbols. Now if, on an average, there are twenty thousand different words in each language or dialect, a person who is acquainted with fifteen languages will have his memory charged with three hundred thousand different words. And it by no means follows that, however mighty and numerous the mental expressions of some individuals may have been, that they have got to the utmost extent of the capabilities of their minds: if the age of the studious man, (providing he remain in a state of mental soundness,) were prolonged to seven hundred years instead of seventy, his mind would be growing increasingly replete with the treasures of wisdom. In a word, the mind can analyse and arrange, not only its own thoughts, but those of others. A thought expressed by one is amplified by another, and is conveyed hither and thither until an entire neighbourhood, and even town, is benefited by it.

It analyses the crust of the earth; it has found out the numberless secret abodes of light; and what will be the achievement of science in ages to come we cannot conceive. In short, mind is seen in everything. From the rude fence encircling the farm, to the most gaily adorned mansion in the land; from the paper boat of a child to the " Great Eastern;" from the rude strokes of the playful child on paper, to the most exquisite paintings of the masters; from the rudest to the most highly finished and complicated machinery; from the lispings of the infant to the powerful orations of Demosthenes, Cicero, and Pericles; from the boy learning the letters of the alphabet to the most refined and varied literary character; and from the noviciate in figures to the greatest mathematician, we learn some little of the capabilities of the mind.

The mind has its physical expressions, which are indications of its strength and power; but this branch of science should be cautiously studied; for, on the one hand, it has been practically demonstrated that individuals possessing a certain conformation of the head, have corresponding mental and moral susceptibilities and powers, as indicated by the several protuberances; and it by no means appears that it is at all improper to judge of the peculiar mental capabilities by these expressions. Moreover, it has been observed by those who have studied the science of the external developments of mind, that certain protuberances have enlarged in proportion as the perceptive or reflective organs indicated by them have been called into requisition.

On the other hand, the danger has been, and still is, to judge of mind too much by these external developments or protuberances, and to apply the same mode of reasoning to them as we do to muscular ability in man and beast. The danger of this is to reduce the science of mind to a materialistic series of propositions. Sufficient has been said on the immateriality of mind to guard us against this error on the present occasion. One part of the danger we have just considered is, that when we make the science of Phrenology unexceptionable, we make the internal affections dependent for their existence on material causes, and, like them, to be mortal. I need not say that this conclusion is at once at variance with the inspired volume, and with daily experience. The mind is capable of undying youth and vigour. Our bodies are subject to the decaying and withering influences induced by the circumstances around and within us : but mind is not measured by years; it knows no decay. As one proof out of many we may cite Cato Major,* who, having several times filled the highest office in the Roman Senate, when an old man commenced the study of Greek, and, from the quotations which he makes in his Conversations with Lælius and Scipio, it is clear that he had not only read a great number of Greek authors, but retained what he had read.

---

* Quid, quod etiam addiscunt aliquid? et Solonem versibus gloriantem, videmus, qui *se*, quotidie aliquid addiscentem, senem fieri dicit : ut ego feci, qui Græcas litteras senex didici; quas quidem sic avide arripui, quasi diuturnam sitim explere Cupiens, ut ea ipsa mihi nota essent, quibus me nunc exemplis uti videtis. Quod quum fecisse Socratem in fidibus audirem, vellem equidem et illud: discebant enim fidibus antiqui : sed in litteris certe elaboravi.　　　Cic. De. Senec. cap. 8.

PART III.

This noble display of the wisdom and goodness of the Infinite, which we have been considering, requires its latent powers and energies to be brought out.

The science of sculpture makes the rude masses in the quarry disclose their hidden beauties. The marble bust or statue once lay concealed amidst heaps of kindred amorphous lumps. No sooner, however, were the instruments of the sculptor brought to operate upon it, than the marble did all but speak. There you see all the lineaments of the features of a sovereign, a warrior, a statesman, or a friend. All the materials composing the magnificent fabrics of Greece, Rome, Egypt, Nineveh, the homes and mansions of our own country, once adorned the forest, or lay embowelled in the earth. The ship, bearing its rich cargo and its hundreds of human beings, was once waving its branches in submission to the winds, and under its shade the weary peasant, the ardent aspirant, or the disconsolate sat. The innumerable gold, and silver utensils, and ornaments had all their materials exhumed from the secret, unseen places of the earth.

That vast continent, in which all the arts of civilized life flourish, was once inhabited by a race of beings—savage and barbarous, but it has been colonised by the intelligent and enterprising, and so its hidden resources have been brought forth from the chambers of oblivion.

Even so is it with mind. It possesses astonishing capabilities and vast resources, but these require to be brought out, and the science which brings them forth is called *Education*.

Before entering fully upon the subject of mental culture, I would respectfully premise that God, who has bestowed upon man such extraordinary powers, holds him responsible for the cultivation, improvement, and use of the same. "That the soul be without knowledge is not good." "There is a spirit in man, and the the inspiration of the Almighty giveth him understanding." Surely we need not make use of a multiplicity of arguments to shew the importance and obligation of mental culture. Do not the history of the past, the requirements of the present, and future anticipations, abundantly convince us of the importance of this duty? Who can visit the dreary solitude of the naturalist or other scientific man, and see the ease and pleasure with which he is whiling away the moments, minutes, hours, days, weeks, and years, by holding intercourse with the treasures of an enriched mind and fertile imagination; or if perchance a beetle or some other insect present itself, it constitutes a volume for the exercise of his mental powers; thus in the enjoyment of ample society, even in his solitude: without feeling that learning is very important to render life pleasant and agreeable, even in the midst of the most unpropitious circumstances? Who can reflect upon the comparative safety with which the miner can descend into the bowels of the earth, and thence bring forth its latent treasures for the use, and comfort of individuals and communities, and not be thankful that the dark days of ignorance are passed away, in which hundreds and thousands were suffocated in the mines? Who can gaze upon the wonderful achievements of art and science, in the infinite variety of simple, and complicated systems of machinery which call forth the skill, and find ample employment for millions of human beings; or, who can reflect upon the comforts of the cottager, contrasted with those of kings in former times, and not be anxious for the extension of mental culture? Who can admire the thousands of mental and social transformations which have and are taking place? Of the man leaving the tending of sheep and becoming an astronomer; of the musician becoming a most profound mathematician, and finding a place in the palaces of kings; of the Northumbrian blacksmith who became learned in the languages and mathematics, &c., and was raised by one of the excellent prelates of our land to have the charge of a parish; or of the great metaphysician of Cornwall, who sprang from the ranks of shoemakers; or of the farm-servant who translated the New Testament into the Feejeean language; or of the boast of Northumberland, who rose from the humblest condition of a collier to be courted by sovereigns and princes; without being desirous for his own education?

Let me now direct your attention to some of the

means to be employed for the attainment of so desirable an object --Mental Culture.

Let me remind you, first of all, to depend principally upon yourselves. There is nothing in the position of any so peculiar that he cannot attend to the improvement of his mind. As it would be vain to commence the study of either science or literature before an individual can read, the first thing to which I shall invite your attention is the importance of reading *intelligently*. To be able to read with ease and intelligence is of paramount importance. I may here remark that, perhaps, the principal reason why some persons do not read so as to profit either themselves or others is because they do not understand the meanings of the words which are used. Now, this difficulty could be surmounted much more easily than such are apt to imagine. If they would take the trouble of referring to a dictionary, or ask some intelligent neighbour or friend, for the purpose of acquiring correct information respecting what they do not at all or fully understand, the irksomeness of reading would be removed, and the advantage and pleasure arising from a slow, careful, and intelligent course of reading would increase day by day. In this way, too, the mind would become enriched and the memory strengthened. Hence it is clear that the reason why some persons do not remember what they have read, or do not take delight in reading, is because they do not understand the different words and phrases which occur.

There is, positively, no excuse for persons not reading intelligently. The sun of intelligence has long ago appeared above the intellectual horizon, scattering the clouds and mists of ignorance; and, if people will but open their eyes and look abroad, they will perceive that the vast treasures of scientific knowledge, and the accumulated wisdom of succeeding ages are opened to them; and that the meandering brooks, and the swelling, widening, and intellectually fertilizing rivers of knowledge are washing away the ignorance and superstition of the past and the vestiges of the present time.

The man who holds communion with the wisdom of past ages, and the discoveries and inventions of the present, is never alone. He may spend the greater part of his life unobserved in a garret, in the midst of some busy city; he may be employed in some country retreat, away from the busy activities of life; but if he can read, he will have a source of pleasure of a far higher and more ennobling nature than the rich simpleton can possibly derive from his coffers filled with gold and silver, and his costly jewels. Yes; the time is even *now* come, when men must go for *what they are as men*, and not for what they appear to be relatively considered.

As to the kind of reading: I would say, and urge upon you by all the sacredness of your intellectual powers, by the unmistakeable indications of the will of the great Moral Governor of the Universe, and by the requirements of the age, read what is TRUTH—plain, unadulterated, honest, historical, scientific, and, above all, and with all the rest, BIBLICAL TRUTH. Settle it

in your minds that nothing is so truly interesting, nothing so attractive, and nothing so substantial as TRUTH.
Man was not intended to feed upon wind; he who,
though finite and depraved, is nevertheless the moral
and intellectual resemblance of the Deity, was never
intended to be the sport of superstition, or of the vile
excogitations of corrupted and filthy imaginations.

Avoid novels and romances, which have nothing to
recommend themselves to your notice but the conceived
or barely probable approximations to truth. Now, if
the semblance of truth is so forcible and fascinating,
what must *Truth* itself be? People may have their
mental powers weakened, their minds poisoned, and
become deranged by reading works of fiction; but they
will never attain to any high intellectual or moral status
by that means.

I view with horror, the demoralizing tendencies and
positively vicious effects which are daily being produced
by the thousands of mere trashy and flashy things which
teem from the great portion of the press. The leading
articles of many periodicals are such as to inflame the
imagination, enkindle the basest feelings, and completely warp and distort the intellectual powers.

Let but the habit of novel reading be once formed,
and there is very little hope of the important branches
of the sciences being prosecuted with vigour and success. I may be reminded, by way of apology or defence
for such reading, of the excellent novels of Knights,
Baronets, Barons, and others. All I have to say

is that I am very sorry that such men should have prostituted their extraordinary talents to such low, grovelling, trashy, poisonous pursuits. " Be not deceived, evil communications corrupt good manners" (or morals).

Read slowly, and, at first, sparingly, if you would remember what you read. Write extracts and make synopses of works of study. This will improve your diction, and give, and enable you to retain, correct notions of the different branches of science which you may be studying. You will really be astonished how much your memory will be improved by this means.

Converse freely about what you are reading and studying. You will by this means gain many new ideas, and become accustomed to express your own views. People who are accustomed to converse about what they are studying, gain additional light upon the different subjects which occupy their attention ; and, while they are thus gaining information, are at the same time imparting knowledge to others. On the other hand, those who converse little improve little, and benefit others very little. The way to increase your stock of knowledge, and become the benefactors of your species, is to communicate to other people what you know. Do not be afraid of making others as wise as yourselves. If you wish to forget what you have read, say nothing about it. I cannot, in this stage of my lecture, do better than make a quotation from Lord Bacon. He says :—" Reading maketh a full man, and writing an exact man, and conference a ready man; and therefore, if a man write little, he had need have a great memory; if he confer little, he had need have a present wit; and if he read little, he had need have much cunning to seem to know that he doth not."

As a means of bringing the mind into a well-disciplined condition, and giving to it that patience which is absolutely necessary in studying the sciences, and tone, vigour, and logical correctness in your expressions, I would recommend the study of the mathematics. It is almost impossible to say too much on the importance of algebra and Euclid. Bacon observes that, " If a man's wits be wandering, let him study the mathematics, for in demonstrations, if his wit be called away ever so little, he must begin again; if his wit be not apt to distinguish or find differences, let him study the schoolmen, for they are 'cumini sectores'—i.e., dividers of Cummin (seed,)" &c. The pure mathematics furnish the architect, engineer, and mechanic, as well as the philosopher, with those infallible data without which their information would be of an exceedingly doubtful character. See the amazing calculations which may be made by algebra. Observe the logical, philosophical, and scientific formulæ with which it furnishes us. How valuable as an assistant to the memory ! Whole pages may be clearly expressed by a few letters. How much more quickly can we pass from the known to a correct knowledge of the unknown by algebra than by the arithmetical process. If persons would make it a more prominent subject of study, their reasoning powers would be daily invigorated; and, instead of pinning themselves to the opinions of others in every trifling matter, they would be able to test the correctness of their premises, and to frame rules for themselves, instead of constantly being dependent upon keys, &c. It may well be termed " THE GREAT ART."

Then I would particularly urge upon you to make the pure and mixed mathematics an important part of your studies. Much as our Universities have thought of their importance hitherto, the feeling is increasing. I cannot leave this part of my lecture without adding a word or two respecting the manner of studying " Euclid's Elements of Geometry." First, do not pass from the definitions of each book before you are thoroughly conversant with them ; then study and remember the postulates and axioms. You will thus find that your mind will be furnished with most important data, without which you cannot proceed with the propositions. Proceed slowly, which is the only way to make real speed. When you begin to demonstrate a proposition, whether it be a problem or theorem, first notice particularly what you are required to do, and then ascertain the data which are supplied ; for example,—I will suppose that you are entering upon the sixth proposition of the first book of Euclid. Well, it is required to prove that if two angles of any triangle are equal, the sides which subtend the equal angles shall be equal also. You must then remember the condition, viz., that there must, in this case, be two equal angles in the triangle; and then, by remembering the two preceding propositions, you will at once, not only see, but also logically demonstrate the proposition. By the fifth proposition you demonstrate the sixth; and by the fourth you show the absurdity of a contrary supposition. If you thus pursue the study of Euclid throughout, you will perceive the beauty, force, and correctness of all his demonstrations; and, at the same time, you will be put in possession of a spirit of patient enquiry, and prepared for the study of other things on correct principles. The importance of arithmetic is so manifest that I need not say anything on that subject.

By attending to the foregoing you will be surprised at the amazing facility with which you will be able to pursue the study of the languages and sciences. The mind, being brought into a state of intellectual fertility, your mental powers will be developed; and there will be every reason to believe that the next generation will far outstrip the present. I cannot help subscribing, to a great extent, to the doctrine of physical, moral, and intellectual heritage. You are, therefore, in duty bound to attend to the cultivation of your minds. Socially and politically considered, mental culture is of paramount importance. There was a time when England was indebted, for her comforts and embellishments, to foreign nations. Now, she possesses resources of her own, by which to enrich many others. Perhaps no country has made such progress in the arts and sciences as she has. A kingdom, possessed of so many seminaries of learning, religious institutions, such as places for public worship, Sabbath schools, Bible Societies, Young Men's Christian Associations, and the like, is destined, by the unerring providence of God, to be great in mind, morals, politics, and religion. Where learning and piety are cultivated, the people are free. Where neither religion nor learning is cultivated, the people are barbarous, and very nearly allied to the brute.

Accustom yourselves to depend upon your own powers. All that can *really* be done for you by persons, books, and lectures is, to assist you to develope your powers, and by removing some real or supposed difficulty, to help you forward to another height. Take it for granted that no person can think and act for you : he may help you to think, and assist you in your studies, but still *you* must think.

A person who is continually being crutched up by others will never excel in any branch of science. The great men of this, as well as of bygone days, made *themselves* so, whether they were students in universities, or had to wend their way through the mazy labyrinths of difficulties. What others have done, *you* may do ; and there is no reason why you should not be ranked amongst the social, moral, and intellectual benefactors of your species. A distinguished member of the University of Edinburgh was, for many years, accustomed to ply his trade for something like thirteen hours a day. The cloud of ignorance and neglect encircled his early years. No sooner, however, did he see the vast importance of mental culture, than he most assiduously applied himself to the study of mathematics and the learned languages. His great proficiency attracted the notice of three literary and wealthy gentlemen, who jointly bore the expenses of his collegiate course. After quitting the University, he entered the ministry, wrote several valuable works, and, after a life of usefulness, he was gathered to the silent home of his fathers. The honour of thus facilitating the development of this truly great man belongs to the town of Sheffield.

Self-respect, self-reliance, diligence, and perseverance, are the great principles by which difficulties are overcome and eminence secured. Do not allow yourselves to be chafed or vexed because your position and circumstances in life do not appear to be so favourable as the position and circumstances of others whom you know. For aught you know, you are in a much better situation than they. It by no means follows that, because an individual can boast of a large collection of books, that he is or will be learned. Many of the world's simpletons have magnificent book cases, and well stocked with exquisitely bound works. Great men have often been men of *few books*. It is well to consider for what branch of science or literature you are the most adapted. There are departments of learning suited to every individual, and he is most likely to ensure success and rise to eminence who prosecutes that which is most suited to his taste and capacity. Amongst painters you find some whose province is landscape, others the human figure, others drapery, &c. Amongst another class you find some who excel in modelling, sculpture, and the like. In well-conducted Mechanics' Institutions, facilities are afforded to all classes and degrees of mind. There the working man has opportunities presented to him for learning all the immediately useful branches of knowledge. Innumerable are the blessings which have already accrued from such institutions. Thousands have been raised by them from the chambers of obscurity, and have become qualified to occupy most important positions in a literary, scientific, and artistic point of view. May the noble list be swelled by hundreds from the several institutions in the Peak of Derbyshire ; and may many Furnesses and Sewards arise as the literary and scientific representatives of struggling but conquering genius !

It is very lamentable that, notwithstanding all the comforts, conveniences, and embellishments of life which, in the all-wise arrangements of our heavenly Benefactor, are furnished by the working classes, any of the so-called aristocracy, and especially any of the middle-class population of the country, should be opposed to the education of the masses. Let the people be shut up in ignorance, and then bigotry, despotism, and religious intolerance will re-appear with all their horrifying virulence. Let the people be educated on right principles in all the useful branches of learning, and then the laws will be respected, and the rights of fellow-citizens protected.

The state has nothing to fear from the advancement of the masses in literature and science; but it has everything to fear from the prevalence of ignorance, superstition, and bigotry. The history of Mechanics' Institutions furnishes abundant proofs in corroboration of the foregoing. Education promotes self-respect, self-reliance, and perseverance; and these are most important qualities, whether socially or nationally considered. I feel persuaded that I cannot do better than close my lecture by making a quotation from Lord Brougham's "Practical Observations upon the Education of the People":—"I rejoice to think that it is not necessary to close these observations by combating objections to the diffusion of science among the working classes, arising from considerations of a political nature. Happily the time is past and gone when bigots could persuade mankind that the lights of philosophy were to be extinguished as dangerous to religion; and when tyrants could proscribe the instructors of the people as enemies to their power. It is preposterous to imagine that the enlargement of our acquaintance with the laws which regulate the universe, can dispose to unbelief. It may be a cure for superstition—for intolerance it will be the most certain cure; but a pure and true religion has nothing to fear from the greatest expansion which the understanding can receive by the study either of matter or of mind. The more widely science is diffused, the better will the Author of all things be known, and the less will the people be ' tossed to and fro by the sleight of men, and cunning craftiness whereby they lie in wait to deceive.' To tyrants, indeed, and- bad rulers, the progress of knowledge among the masses of mankind is a just object of terror: it is fatal to them and their designs; they know this by unerring instinct, and unceasingly they dread the light. But they will find it more easy to curse than to extinguish. It is spreading in spite of them, even in those countries where arbitrary power deems itself most secure; and in England, any attempt to check its progress would only bring about the sudden destruction of him who should be insane enough to make it."

ROBERT LEADER, PRINTER, INDEPENDENT OFFICE, SHEFFIELD.